STECK-VAUGHN

PAIR-IT BOOKS™

Sandwiches, Sandwiches

Written by Jeffrey Stoodt

STECK-VAUGHN®
C O M P A N Y
ELEMENTARY • SECONDARY • ADULT • LIBRARY

A sandwich can be very tall.

A sandwich can be very small.

A sandwich can be made with meat.

A sandwich can be very sweet.

A sandwich can be stuffed just right.

A sandwich can be dark or light.

But the sandwich I most like to eat
is a peanut butter and banana treat!